by Eric Maher & Mark Poulton

An American Wolf in London, Another Eddie Edwards Story.

Copyright © 2020 by Eric Maher and Mark Poulton

Written by
Eric Maher with Mark Poulton

Illustrated by
Mark Poulton

Colored & Lettered by
Dexter Weeks

All Rights Reserved.
No part of this publication may be reproduced or transmitted in any form or by any means, electronic or mechanical, including photocopy, recording, or any information storage and retrieval system, without permission in writing from the publisher.

For information regarding permission, write to:
Sevenhorns Publishing
Attention: Permissions
276 5th Avenue, Suite 704
New York, New York 10001

Published by
www.sevenhornspublishing.com

Design Support: Branded Human

Library of Congress Control Number: 2021930541

ISBN: 978-1-7363887-2-3

Printed in the U.S.A.

www.sevenhornspublishing.com

To "Lil' Poopy"
You are more than we ever expected
and better than we ever imagined
—Eddie

To my little monster, Chase
—Mark

Thank you to Kim, Alanna, and Sofia
—Dexter

HOLD THE NEXT PAGE BY THE LOWER CORNER AND FLIP IT BACK AND FORTH TO CREATE WEREWOLF ACTION!

DID YOU KNOW EDDIE IS A TWO TIME IMPACT WRESTLING WORLD CHAMPION, TWO TIME X-DIVISION CHAMPION AND FIVE TIME TAG TEAM CHAMPION (AS PART OF THE AMERICAN WOLVES)?

BONUS PIN UP BY COMIC LEGEND, *RON WILSON!*

ANOTHER EDDIE EDWARDS STORY

by Eric Maher & Mark Poulton

www.sevenhornspublishing.com

Follow Eddie Edwards @TheEddieEdwards   Follow Mark Poulton @koniwaves
Follow Dexter Weeks @ dexter_art
Follow Sevenhorns Publishing @sevenhornsbooks

BONUS PIN UP BY, *MARK MARIANELLI!*

An American Wolf in London
Another Eddie Edwards Story

by Eric Maher & Mark Poulton

SEVEN HORNS PUBLISHING

www.sevenhornspublishing.com

Follow Eddie Edwards @TheEddieEdwards   Follow Mark Poulton @koniwaves
Follow Dexter Weeks @ dexter_art
Follow Sevenhorns Publishing @sevenhornsbooks

BONUS PIN UP BY, MARK YOON!

An American Wolf in London
Another Eddie Edwards Story

by Eric Maher & Mark Poulton

SEVEN HORNS PUBLISHING

www.sevenhornspublishing.com

Follow Eddie Edwards @TheEddieEdwards   Follow Mark Poulton @koniwaves
Follow Dexter Weeks @ dexter_art
Follow Sevenhorns Publishing @sevenhornsbooks

BONUS PIN UP BY, MARK POULTON!

AN AMERICAN WOLF IN LONDON
ANOTHER EDDIE EDWARDS STORY

by Eric Maher & Mark Poulton

www.sevenhornspublishing.com

Follow Eddie Edwards @TheEddieEdwards   Follow Mark Poulton @koniwaves
Follow Dexter Weeks @ dexter_art
Follow Sevenhorns Publishing @sevenhornsbooks

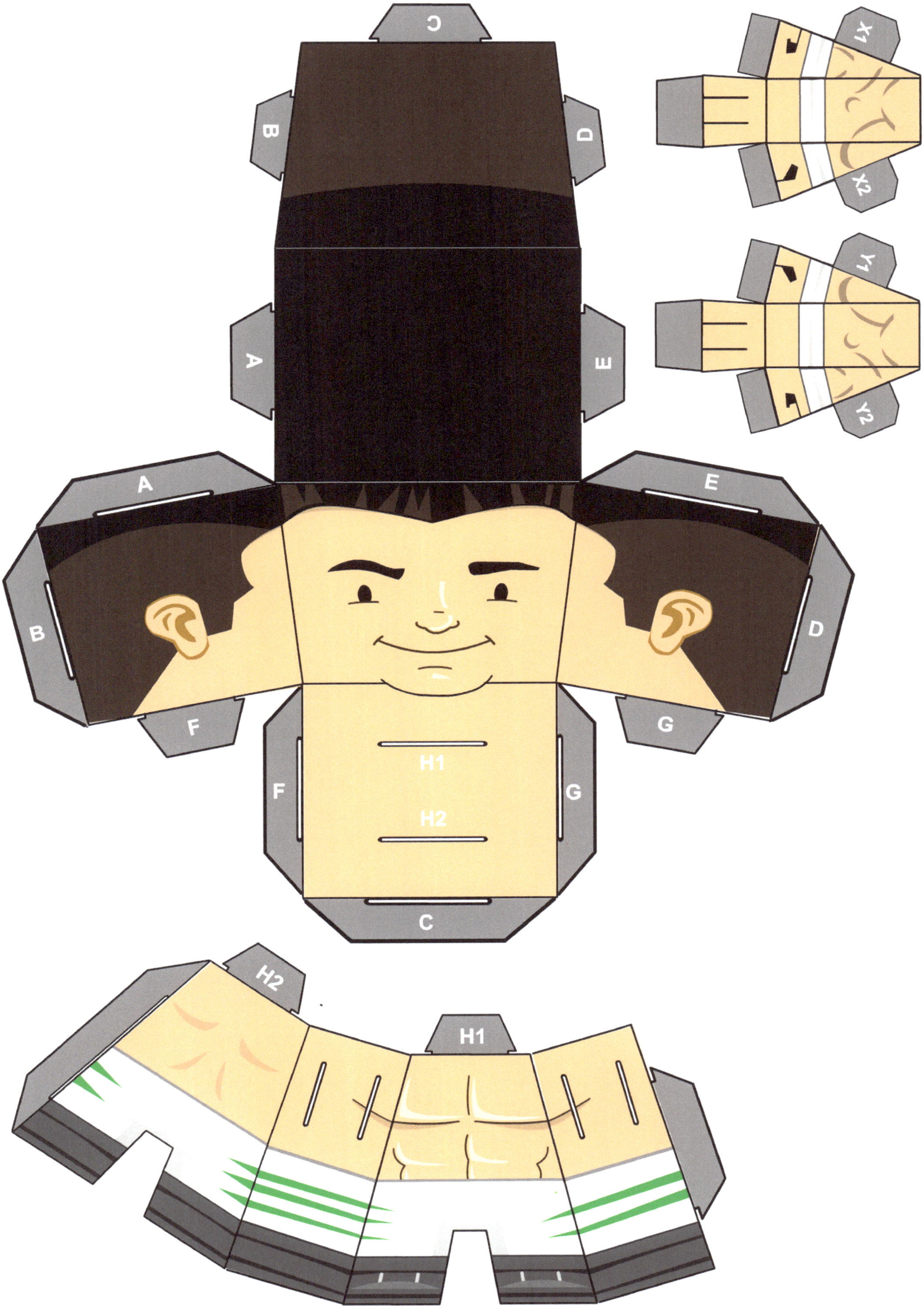
C
B
D
A
E
X1
X2
Y1
Y2
A
E
B
D
F
G
H1
H2
F
G
C
H2
H1

AN AMERICAN WOLF IN LONDON
ANOTHER EDDIE EDWARDS STORY

by Eric Maher & Mark Poulton

www.sevenhornspublishing.com

Follow Eddie Edwards @TheEddieEdwards   Follow Mark Poulton @koniwaves
Follow Dexter Weeks @ dexter_art
Follow Sevenhorns Publishing @sevenhornsbooks

BONUS PIN UP BY, PHIL MCNULTY!